THE TRUTH

P J Gray

SADDLEBACK
PUBLISHING

COMING HOME
BOOK 3

COMING HOME

SEARCHING FOR ANSWERS

THE TRUTH

SADDLEBACK
P U B L I S H I N G
www.sdlback.com

ISBN-13: 978-1-62250-053-6
ISBN-10: 1-62250-053-9
eBook: 978-1-61247-711-4

Printed in Guangzhou, China
NOR/0313/CA21300351

17 16 15 14 13   1 2 3 4 5

Author
Acknowledgments

I wish to thank Carol Senderowitz for her friendship and belief in my abilities. I wish to thank Linnea Johnson for her inspiration and dedication to learning. Additional thanks and gratitude to my family and friends for their love and support; likewise to the staff at Saddleback Educational Publishing for their generosity, graciousness, and enthusiasm. Most importantly, my heartfelt thanks to Scott Drawe for his love and support.

The Bottom of the Stairs

Nia could not wait to tell Karyn the truth.

She was ready to tell Karyn that she was Will's mother.

She was also ready to tell Karyn that she was happy about the baby.

Nia entered the nail shop. She did not see Karyn.

"Hello! Is anyone here?" Nia called out.

The shop looked empty.

"Why is the front door open when nobody is here?" Nia asked herself.

Nia walked to the back room. She did not see anyone.

She could feel that something was very wrong.

She walked to the back door.

Nia called out again, "Hello! Is anyone here?"

The shop was quiet.

Then Nia saw the open basement door.
She walked to it. The basement was dark.
Nia heard a moan.

"What was that sound? Hello! Is anyone
down there?"

She turned on the light. "Why are there towels here?" she thought.

Then she saw Karyn lying at the bottom of the stairs.

She was not moving.

Nia screamed, "Karyn!"

The Big Silver Car

Will tried to wait for Karyn to finish work. But he could not wait.

He had to follow the big silver car.

He followed it across town.

The car stopped at the Burger Joint.

Will stopped across the street and waited.

Eve stepped out. She walked into the restaurant.

Will waited.

Eve walked out of the restaurant with Toby.

Will was shocked.

Toby got into the car with Eve. They drove away.

Will followed them to Toby's house.

Will called Toby on his cell phone.

Toby answered.

Will said, "Hey, it's Will. Where are you?"

"I'm with a friend. We are at the mall."

"Okay, I'll talk to you later," Will said. He hung up his cell phone.

Will was very mad. He knew that Toby lied.

Will watched Eve and Toby enter Toby's house.

Help Is Coming

Nia looked down at Karyn and screamed,
"Karyn! Can you hear me?"

Nia pulled out her cell phone.

She dialed 911.

"This is nine-one-one," the operator said.

"I need help right now! Hurry!" Nia said.

"Where are you?"

"I'm in a nail shop at one fifty-four Barry Street," Nia said.

"Are you hurt?" the operator asked.

"No, my friend Karyn is hurt. She fell down the stairs. She's not answering me."

"Have you moved her?" the operator asked.

"No! Hurry! Please hurry! We are at one fifty-four Barry Street."

Nia hung up. She ran down the stairs to Karyn.

She put her hand on Karyn's face.

Nia asked, "Karyn? Karyn? Can you hear me?"

Karyn opened her eyes slowly.

Nia was so happy. She smiled at Karyn.

"Can you hear me?" Nia asked.

"Yes," Karyn replied.

"I called nine-one-one, Karyn. They're coming," Nia said with tears in her eyes.

Karyn cried, "My baby. My baby."

Her eyes closed. She did not move.

Nia sobbed, "Karyn!"

Just then, Nia could hear the sirens.

News for Gail

Gail had been taking care of her granddaughter for five years.

Her granddaughter, Jada, lived with her.

She took care of Jada while Carl traveled for his job.

Carl came home after a long trip.
He was tired.

He had to share some news with Gail.

"Mother, we have to talk," Carl said to Gail.

Gail put Jada down for a nap. She went to sit with Carl in the kitchen.

Carl said, "Mother, I got a new job."

"That is very good news," Gail answered.

"The new job is far away," Carl said.

"Do you want me to keep Jada here?" Gail asked.

"No, Mother. I want to take Jada with me. I won't be traveling anymore."

"No! You cannot take her from me," Gail said. "She doesn't know you."

"Don't get mad, Mother."

"No, Carl! You cannot take her from me. She is my life."

Gail began to cry.

Carl put his hand on her arm.

Gail stood up and walked to her bedroom.

Truth from the Window

Will watched Eve and Toby enter Toby's house.

He left his car across the street. He walked to the side of the house.

Will moved softly to a window.

He did not want Toby or Eve to see him.

He slowly looked into the house. He could hear them talking.

Will saw Eve and Toby sitting together.

He saw many guns on a table. There were big guns and small guns.

Eve said, "Shawn wants his money now."

"He's crazy. He owes *me* money," Toby replied.

"Then you talk to him," Eve said.

Will stepped away from the window.

He walked quietly back to his car.

Will was very mad. He knew that they killed Mike.

He wanted to kill them.

He looked at his watch. It was seven o'clock.

Karyn would be calling him.

Suddenly Will's cell phone rang. It was Nia.

"Will!" Nia said.

"Mama, I can't talk right now," Will said.

"Come to the hospital right away!"

"Why? What's wrong?" Will asked.

Nia said, "It's Karyn. She's hurt."

A Mother Is Loved

Carl knocked on Gail's bedroom door.

She did not answer.

He opened the door.

Gail was sitting on her bed.

She was looking out of her bedroom window.

"Mother, don't be mad," Carl said.

"I cannot live without Jada," Gail replied.

"I know."

"You gave her to me. Now you want to take her away," Gail said.

"Yes, but I want you to come with us."

"What?" Gail said.

Carl sat down next to her and held her hand.

"I said that I want you to move with us. I will buy a big house for all of us," Carl said gently.

Gail said, "I don't know, Carl. I have lived here for so long."

"I know, Mother. Please come with us. We both love you very much."

Gail smiled at Carl.

He kissed her face and wiped away a tear.

"Grandma! Grandma!" Jada said as she stood at the bedroom door.

The Policemen Hear the Truth

Will and Nia waited in the hospital.

Karyn had been with the doctors for over two hours.

Two policemen found them sitting in the waiting room.

Nia told the policemen about Karyn and the stairs.

Will told the policemen about Eve and the big silver car.

He also told them about Toby and the guns.

"Where is the house?" one of the policemen asked Will.

Will answered, "Seven twenty-five West River Street."

The other policeman called the police station for more help.

The policemen thanked Nia and Will. Then they hurried to their cars.

A doctor saw Nia and Will.

He said, "Karyn is badly hurt."

Will asked, "Will she be okay?"

"I don't know yet," the doctor replied. "We are doing the best we can."

The doctor walked away.

Nia looked at Will and said, "I know about the baby."

"I love Karyn," Will said.

"I know you do, son."

"And I want to be a father," Will said.

Shoot to Kill

The policemen went to Toby's house.

The policemen looked inside the window and saw all of the guns.

They saw Eve on her cell phone. She was biting her fingernails.

They saw Toby sitting on an old, dirty sofa.

Eve called her brother, Shawn.

Shawn would not answer his phone.

He had been hiding in another city since the murder of Will's father, Mike.

Shawn owed Toby money.

Toby owed Shawn money.

They had both lost track of how much.
And now both were mad.

"Tell Shawn he owes me. I want my money
now or no deal," Toby yelled at Eve.

"He won't answer his phone," Eve yelled back.
"You try calling."

"Your brother has been like this since
high school," Toby yelled. "You can never
trust him!"

Toby saw the policemen through the window.

"Cops!" Toby jumped up from the sofa and grabbed a gun.

Eve fell to the floor and dropped her cell phone.

"Come out with your hands up," a policeman yelled from outside of the house.

Toby fired his gun. *Bang. Bang. Bang.*

He would not come out of the house.

After many hours, Eve came out of the house with her hands up.

Toby was shot and killed in the house.

Eve was sent to jail for a very long time.

The police were still looking for her brother, Shawn.

Turning It All Around

Toby was dead. Eve was in jail. Shawn was a wanted man.

Will went back to work at the factory, but he wanted a better job.

One day a policeman saw Will at the Burger Joint.

He was the policeman from the shooting at Toby's house.

He sat down at Will's table and ate lunch with him.

They talked a long time.

They talked about Toby and Eve and the shooting.

They talked about jobs and family.

They talked about life.

"You should think about joining the police force," he told Will. "You would make a really good cop."

Will told Karyn about his lunch with
the policeman.

Will liked the idea, and Karyn was happy.

Will studied a lot.

He worked out.

And he got accepted to the police training
program.

Will spent four months in training.

It was hard work. But he was happy and did very well.

Will finished at the top of his class.

A New Start

Carl was ready to start his new job.

He was happy to bring Gail and Jada with him.

Gail was happy to go with Carl and Jada.

They were her family. She loved them.

Gail was sad about selling her house.

She'd lived in that house for many years.

Gail was also sad about leaving Nia.

Nia was her best friend and neighbor.

How was she going to say good-bye to her best friend?

Gail packed the moving boxes and cried.

"It will be okay, Mother," Carl said. "You'll like the new house."

"I know, son," Gail replied.

"And the new house has a big backyard for Jada."

The last boxes were packed. The house was quiet.

There was a knock on the front door.

Gail knew who it was. It was Nia.

Now Gail had to say good-bye.

Nothing but the Truth

A year has passed.

Karyn was better. It took her many months.

She lost the baby from the fall down
the stairs.

The doctors said that she might be able
to have another baby.

Will and Karyn got married.

They are very happy together.

Will is a policeman now. He likes his job.

Karyn works at a new nail shop. She feels better and is getting stronger every day.

She wants to buy her own shop one day.

Will and Karyn are trying to have another baby.

Gail sold her house. Will and Karyn bought it.

Now they live next door to Nia.

Nia likes to help Karyn make the house look pretty.

Gail, Carl, and Jada are very happy in their new home.

Gail talks to Nia a lot on the phone. Nia plans to visit her soon.

Nia is very happy now.

Nia still goes to Karyn to get her nails done.

And she still works at the factory.

She has a picture of Mike on her desk.

She also has a picture of Will and Karyn
on her desk.

She smiles at the pictures every day.

About the Author

PJ Gray is a versatile, award-winning freelance writer experienced in short stories, essays, and feature writing. He is a former managing editor for *Pride* magazine, a ghost writer, blogger, researcher, food writer, and cookbook author. He currently resides in Chicago, Illinois. For more information about PJ Gray, go to www.pjgray.com.